Lark Eden

an epistolary play

by

Natalie Symons

Booktrope Editions
Seattle WA
2011

Copyright © Natalie Symons 2011

Cover Design: Simanson Design (simansondesign.com)

ISBN 978-1-935961-07-9

DISCOUNTS OR CUSTOMIZED EDITIONS MAY BE AVAILABLE FOR EDUCATIONAL AND OTHER GROUPS BASED ON BULK PURCHASE.

For further information please contact info@libertary.com

Library of Congress Control Number: 2011905224

Lark Eden was originally presented by Theater Schmeater (J.D. Lloyd, artistic director; Teri Lazzara, managing director) in Seattle, Washington, on April 29th, 2011. It was directed by Douglas Staley. The cast was as follows:

Thelma...................................Teri Lazzara

Mary......................................Tess Hardwick

Emily.....................................Natalie Symons

AUTHOR'S NOTE

When I set out to write *Lark Eden* I did so with the intent of writing an epistolary novel. However, as the story began to take shape it became apparent that the rhythm and texture of the language demanded a voice, or rather three distinct female voices. I soon realized that I was not writing a novel but instead a score for voice. Three speaking voices that move, not across the page, but instead run and rise and fall across time – voices that serve as the cadence of time, caving into one another as time collapses into memory. Perhaps it's my theatre background that led to the development of *Lark Eden* as such; nevertheless I wanted it to be deliberate in its use of voice. With this in mind, what follows is an epistolary play to be performed by three women of approximately the same age. It is a work of which can be given a formal theatrical staging, or to reinstate the Victorian practice of family reading, it may require only that three women commit to an evening of reading the play aloud. In either case I offer these suggestions: The women sit at a non-descript kitchen table and read the letters aloud. They listen to each other and respond as if they are in the same room. That is, the dialogue is intended to be treated with a sense of immediacy and not as if it is coming from a far off place. Where indicated, the dialogue does not come to complete stops. The voices ought to fade in and out of each other – never halting, but rather blurring and wilting into one another, much in the same way as our memories do.

ACT ONE

THELMA:

Dear Mary. That Elmer Carmichael is a pest. He drops his pencil on purpose so he can get down on his knees and look up Miss Benner's skirt. I find him to be rude and vulgar.

MARY:

You just wish he was looking up your skirt.

THELMA:

Mary Ann Marie, you are the one who is vulgar and rude.

EMILY:

Stop passing notes to each other. Ya'll are distracting me.

MARY:

Don't be so darn serious Em. You're ruining my fun.

THELMA:

I will not pass notes in school…

MARY:

I will not pass notes in school…

EMILY:

I will not pass notes in school, I will not pass notes in school, I will not pass notes in school. (cont'd)

*   *   *

EMILY:

You are invited to attend my 12th birthday party at 12:00 in the afternoon on Saturday March 3rd, 1935 at 28 Waters Lane. Lark Eden, Georgia.

MARY:

I regret to tell you that I will be unable to attend your birthday party because Ma says we don't have enough money to buy you a proper birthday present. I'm sorry Em.

EMILY:

I don't need a silly present. You're my best friend. I don't even want to have the dumb party if you can't come. Tell your mother there are no presents allowed.

MARY:

Ma still says no.

EMILY:

Dear Thelma. Thank you for Shirley Temple's Birthday Book. I am enjoying the variety of paper dolls and dresses. I hope that you had a nice time at my party.

*   *   *

MARY:

Greetings from Huntsville, Alabama. I'm here with Ma helping my old grandmother Harriet recover from her fall. Apparently she was already impossibly old when she gave birth to my mother, so you can imagine what she looks like now. The first time I laid eyes on her all crippled in her bed a chill ran up my spine – just like the time I was swimming in the pond near Martha Miller's house and something bit my foot. She fixed me with a little grin and I counted seven teeth – four on top and three on the bottom – just hanging there out of her gums.

EMILY:

Is she going to be okay Mary?

MARY:

I swear to sweet Jesus, just an effortless tug could remove those teeth from her head.

EMILY:

Will you be coming home soon?

MARY:

She looks like she was ridden hard and put up wet. Like the sort of woman who picks and cans and slaughters things with her own hands.

THELMA:

Be kind Mary...

MARY:

I sincerely hope that I don't have nightmares after being exposed to the sight and sound of the old lady. She's given to bouts of dislodging something from her throat and then she swallows whatever it is that comes up. Emphysema or cancer of the lung is what it sounds like to me.

THELMA:

Mary don't be vulgar...

MARY:

Yesterday she caught me in her milky stare and said, "Let me get a look at you. Well look at that, you got little bosoms already." Then she made me sit on the bed with her and she groped my face with her surprisingly strong fingers and kept telling me how much I looked like Ma. Her fingers remind me very much of chicken bones – all knobby and brittle looking.

THELMA:

May God be with you always Mary, and your grandmother too.

EMILY:

Do you think she'll ever walk again?

MARY:

She broke both her hips and shattered her kneecap. She better walk again – I want to get out of here. Her house smells like boiled meat.

THELMA:

Be kind Mary…

MARY:

Did I mention what her breath smells like?

THELMA:

She's in my prayers…

MARY:

It's foul from being trapped inside that woman. First time I got a whiff, almost immediately I had visions of when I was eight and that raccoon crawled under our house and died. I can't take another minute of the old lady whacking her cane on the floor and ordering me to fetch her prune juice. Her face looks like a prune if you ask me – all squished and purple.

EMILY:

Guess what? Elmer Carmichael tried to hold Thelma's hand outside Jack Dundin's father's hardware store.

MARY:

See what I'm missing ya'll. Is our sweet patootie Thelma getting cozy with Elmer?

THELMA:

You are full of malarkey Mary Ann Marie.

MARY:

Why Miss Thelma, are you blushing over there? I think you and Elmer are cute as a bug's ear together.

THELMA:

Oh for goodness sake, will ya'll leave me alone please.

MARY:

Good news I'm coming home. I told Ma I need to go home and watch after Daddy. He telegrammed and said his cough is worse. Abyssinia!

*   *   *

THELMA:

Dear Emily. Thank you for sending me the picture of Clark Gable and Jean Harlow. She was way too young to die, God rest her soul. Emily, please forgive me for asking this, but why is it that you never sing in church? I can see you over there with your lips pursed into that perfect little O shape you make and your eyes narrowed into mean slits that look as though they could cut right through a person. What's wrong with you Em?

EMILY:

I'm just not much in the mood for any of it to tell you the truth. All that singing and chanting at the Lord like he gives a hoot what happens down here, well I just think it's silly that's all. To be quite honest, I think He's got too much on his plate to be concerned about the people in this little town. That old traffic sign may read 15 miles per hour, but most people just speed on by. God probably forgets that Lark Eden is even here half of the time. So please leave me alone Thelma, I'm not going to sing just because everyone else is.

THELMA:

Now don't go attacking the Lord. I was just wondering why your face was so pinched.

EMILY:

If God cared so much, why did he let Mary's father get so sick?

MARY:

Don't worry about my father Em. The Doc says he should be better in no time. They think they caught it before it spread to his lungs. Besides it's Ma that I'm the most worried about. She cries all the time and says that we don't have any money – says it will take an act of God to get out from under the heap of doctors bills that we're acquiring.

THELMA:

I'll pray Mary.

*   *   *

MARY:

Dear Thelma. If there was ever someone to play the Blessed Mary it is you. I thought you looked very natural holding the baby Jesus in the Christmas Pageant. You looked just like I imagined her to be – very motherly – and thin. (cont'd)

*   *   *

MARY:

Dear Emily. It is very possible that Miss Wally was attractive once, but now I think she looks like W.C. Fields, don't you?

EMILY:

Stop passing notes to me.

MARY:

It's uncanny don't you think?

EMILY:

Stop.

MARY:

I'm serious Em, look at her up there. She's a tough little nugget of a woman – nearly bald-headed like a man.

EMILY:

Stop.

MARY:

Poor lady took a long dip in the ugly pond.

EMILY:

Please stop.

MARY:

Uglier than homemade sin.

EMILY:

I think that Miss Wally is a very lonesome person. I can tell by her eyes that she's covering up the lonesomeness that she doesn't want anyone to see. Like she's slow dancing with no one is what it looks like to me. So I think you should be nice.

MARY:

Lighten up Emily. I'm just trying to have some fun. Why do you always have to be so gloomy?

* * *

THELMA:

Merry Christmas to my two best friends. May the Lord be with you.

* * *

MARY:

Happy 1939! Yes Emily, happy! You should be happy. You can't solve the world's problems with all your gloom and doom Em.

EMILY:

I don't see how anyone can be happy at a time like this Mary Ann Marie. Our involvement in the war is only a matter of time. I can't help but worry about the boys in this town having to go over there...

MARY:

Can we worry about it later and try to have some fun for once in our lives...

* * *

EMILY:

Dear Mary. I'm writing because I'm too mad to say this to your face without getting too flustered to say what I need to say. For a person who says that they're my best friend you certainly don't act like it sometimes. As you are aware, I think I may be in love with Sammy Wiener. How could you kiss him on New Years Eve behind the Picard's tool shed? Did you think I wouldn't find out about it? Thelma told me that your makeup involved heavy amounts of pink rouge and lipstick and that you talked differently than you usually do to boys. She said your voice went high pitched and you laughed at every other word he said to you. And then you disappeared for an hour and came back with the lipstick all over your face, and that you smelled like alcohol. I'm so mad at you Mary Ann Marie. When I don't speak to you at school, now you will know why.

MARY:

Dear Emily. I'm very sorry that I hurt your feelings. You're right I'm a horrible rotten friend. I don't know why I did it. I understand if you don't want to speak to me. I'll give you as much time as you need to forgive me for my evilness.

EMILY:

Do you love him?

MARY:

No.

EMILY:

What was it like kissing him?

MARY:

Wet.

*　　*　　*

THELMA:

Dear Mary. My prayers and thoughts are with you and your mother. I have asked the Lord to watch over you during this difficult time. It was a beautiful service. I thought that the eulogy that Father Thomas delivered was lovely. God be with you Mary, and your mother too. Love, Thelma

EMILY:

Dear Mary. Your father's funeral service was very sad. I got melancholy looking at the shiny toes of that Jesus statue poking out from under his robe. They gave me a gloomy feeling. I

listened Mary. I listened hard to the words of
Father Thomas. And frankly I thought it
sounded rehearsed. Why don't folks say it like
it is? All those whispered condolences and
glum faces that people wear. And the low pipe
of that organ humming away, it seems to me
it's all just a way for folks to avoid saying
what's really on their minds. If we started
saying it like it is, we could avoid these phony
affairs all together. Life's not very kind is it
Mary? I will pray for you and your mother,
down on my knees with my palms pressed
together, the way Thelma told me that the Lord
likes to receive his prayers.

THELMA:

Dear Mary. I miss you. I know what a hard
time this is for you and your mother. The Lord
works in mysterious ways and it is hard
sometimes to see that he has a purpose for us...

EMILY:

Mary I'm worried about you. You haven't been
in school in nearly two weeks...

THELMA:

Dear Mary. Are you all right? I've been on my
knees twice as long every night asking God to
watch over you...

EMILY:

I stopped by your house today and your mother said you weren't home. She was very tired looking and her hair was dirty...

THELMA:

Here are all of the math assignments that you've been missing. Miss Wally said that I should help you catch up...

EMILY:

Mary, where are you?

THELMA:

God has a plan for us Mary...

EMILY:

I stopped by your house again today. No one was home...

MARY:

Stop. Stop coming over Emily. God has a plan all right Thelma – to kill my father and leave me alone with Ma while she moans about her miserable life. His plan stinks. Emily's right, God's got too much on his mind to watch after the people in this dumb town. And I don't want the stupid math assignments either. I'm not coming back to school. (cont'd)

*   *   *

MARY:

Greetings from Happyville – I mean Huntsville. Ma hasn't gotten out of bed since we got here. She says she has the Blues. So on account of Ma being Blue I'm stuck being nursemaid to Harriet who, I might add, is looking more and more prune-faced with each passing minute. Her skin is alarmingly loose, all stretched and wrinkled. Even more alarming are those fingers, fingers so twisted it's like they are meant for a monster. At least the old bag can walk now. I miss Daddy.

THELMA:

It won't be the same without you here Mary. I don't care what your mother says, I think you should finish school.

MARY:

Old Harriet is in the habit of shouting orders from her bedroom. She gives the floor a blubbery smack with that cane of hers and hollers "Mary, you help your mother with the dishes. Mary, don't forget to brush your teeth" – which strikes me as an odd command, being that the last time that woman took a toothbrush to her mouth was when Grover Cleveland was president. I miss my best friends.

EMILY:

Mary, we miss you more than you will ever know. I cannot believe you have to live there now. I wrote a poem for you. Here it is:

There is a place where the lark sings.
It's a place between all it is that you hope for
And all it is that you have.
Between tomorrow and today
Between dream and wake
This is the place where the song
of the larks can be heard in our Eden.

MARY:

It's beautiful Em, but what does it have to do with me?

EMILY:

The place in the poem *is* you Mary.

MARY:

Bless your pea pickin' heart...

THELMA:

Now look what you've done Miss Mary, you've turned our Em into Shakespeare. She's writing sonnets.

EMILY:

It's not a sonnet.

MARY:

I love it Em. I love you both. More to come from the House of Happy later. Your dear old friend Mary Ann Marie

* * *

THELMA:

Dear Mary. I'm writing to tell you before you hear it from Emily. I think George Rikowski is going to ask for my hand in Holy Matrimony. I must admit, that it has all happened rather quickly. It was only two months ago that we first held hands. George says he can't wait another minute longer to have me as his wife. He makes a face like he's going to burst whenever he says it. Mary, you're the first person that I wanted to tell. Your dearest friend, the soon to be Mrs. George Rikowski

* * *

EMILY:

Can you believe it Mary? George Rikowski got down on one knee and proposed to Thelma after church on Sunday. Our Thelma is getting married!

*　　*　　*

THELMA:

Dear Mary. The wedding will be March 10th. That means that in less than a three months you and Emily will be my bridesmaids.

*　　*　　*

EMILY:

Dear Mary. Is everything all right over there? I'm worried about you. Thelma says she hasn't heard a peep from you about her wedding.

*　　*　　*

THELMA:

Are you getting my letters Mary? Please write or call.

EMILY:

Mary where are you?

*   *   *

THELMA:

Mr. and Mrs. Bernard Williams request the pleasure of your presence at the marriage of their daughter Thelma Bernice to George Eric Rikowski at one o'clock in the afternoon on March 10th, 1941 at Saint Peter's Catholic Church, Abercorn Street, Lark Eden, Georgia.

MARY:

I think you're too young to get married. There I said it. If you have to do this, well of course I'll be there. I love you Thel. P.S. Don't do it.

THELMA:

I will be eighteen next week Mary. And my father has given his blessing. Now all that's left is asking the blessing of the Lord upon this union.

MARY:

Do you love him?

THELMA:

What kind of question is that Mary Ann?

MARY:

Do you love him?

THELMA:

Of course I do. Besides what has that got to do with anything? I want lots of babies Mary, and I am quite certain that George Rikowski will be a wonderful father. (cont'd)

* * *

THELMA:

Dear Emily. Thank you for the salt and peppershakers. George and I will think of you every time we give them a shake. Thank you for being part of the happiest day of my life. God bless you Em. Love, Mr. and Mrs. George Rikowski

EMILY:

Thelma I thought your wedding was a lovely affair. You looked just like Jean Harlow in your wedding dress, particularly when you walked into the church and the sun shone behind you and reflected on your hair.

THELMA:

Thank you Em. I'm not sure about the Jean Harlow part, but you're sweet to say so. What happened to Mary? The last I saw of her she was dancing the Jitterbug with George's cousin Paul and then she vanished. She wasn't even there to catch the bouquet.

MARY:

Hi-de-ho. Back in Happyville. I have wonderful news. I'm getting married to Paul Rikowski. I know it's quick, but I think I'm in love. Just teasing.

THELMA:

What happened to you?

MARY:

Well Thelma, let's just say that I am no longer the virgin Mary.

THELMA:

Shame on you Mary Ann.

EMILY:

Where did you and Paul Rikowski go off to Mary?

MARY:

My dear Emily. First we went for a walk on the beach under a slice of moon and a sprinkle of dancing stars. We recited poetry and discovered the secret of life and then, well the rest is not meant for your virgin ears to hear Miss Emily.

THELMA:

Tell me Mary do you like Paul, even a little bit?

MARY:

Well I did, until he up-chucked on my shoes.

* * *

EMILY:

Life isn't very kind is it Mary? I can't stop crying. I knew that the day would come when we would be forced to get involved in this war. I'm crying for the boys who died on that ship in the harbor. I'm crying for the boys who will die when they are taken from us. I'm crying because there is so much wickedness in the world. I wish that this were just a nightmare that...

* * *

MARY:

You got your wish Thel. Emily told me the news. How far along are you?

*   *   *

THELMA:

On July 18th 1942 at 5:14 in the afternoon the Lord blessed us with a beautiful baby girl. Elizabeth Margaret Rikowski was 7 pounds 4 ounces.

*   *   *

EMILY:

Dear Mary. George received orders. He's going over there to fight. How could God take him away from his baby girl?

*   *   *

THELMA:

Mary, I'm writing to tell you that Elmer Carmichael and George's cousin Paul Rikowski are being deployed next week. Elmer says he is not even the least bit scared. He says he will do whatever it takes to win this war. I'm not sure I believe the part about not being scared. I pray that God will watch over him. I just thought you might want to know – about Paul that is.

*   *   *

EMILY:

Mary, are you coming to Elizabeth's first birthday party? Thelma keeps asking if you're coming…

*   *   *

THELMA:

The party wasn't the same without you Mar. We all missed you…

*   *   *

EMILY:

My Dearest Mary. I am sorry to be the one to have to tell you this, but Paul Rikowski was killed in France. He died on a beach. Just think of it Mary, you held hands on a beach and then he died on a beach. It's the saddest thing I've ever heard in my entire life. I wrote a poem for him. Here it is:

On a beach the wind blew
And the whistles of soldiers
could be heard here that there.
The whistles of a time not long ago…

MARY:

Thelma I am truly sorry to hear about the death of Paul. He was a fine young man. The world will be a sadder place without him...

EMILY:

When life sang and death was a whisper.
Now all that's left is the shadows
of boys gone too soon.
And the songs of the larks in our Eden...

THELMA:

God rest his soul.

MARY:

Thelma I really am sorry. I want you to...

THELMA:

Mary, George is coming home. My husband is coming home to me...

*   *   *

EMILY:

Oh Mary you will never believe it? Thelma is having another...

*   *   *

MARY:

Congratulations on the birth of baby Paul. My golly Thel, you and George are getting all it is that you hoped for, a big happy family...

THELMA:

Thank you Mary. We are truly blessed. The Lord has...

MARY:

Speaking of a big happy family, Ma sends her love, and Old Prune-face Harriet has got gout. So now she has enormous swollen purple feet to match her purple face.

*   *   *

THELMA:

My dearest Mary, George and I want you to be Paul's godmother.

*   *   *

EMILY:

Dear Mary. It was wonderful to see you at the christening of baby Paul. Mar, I hate to say this but you look terrible. I worry that you spend too much time taking care of your mother and that grumpy old grandmother. And now you're working two different jobs. The one in the chemical war manufacturing plant sounds simply awful Mary. You looked a fright with those dark circles under your eyes. You're only twenty-three years old and by the looks of you – well you look forty-three. Please take care of yourself Mary. Love, Emily

MARY:

Now Em, don't you worry your pretty head about me. I'm doing just fine over here at the House of Happy. Since Prune-face got the gout she's given to squawking like a newly hatched bird in her bed. "Mary get me my glasses, Mary Ann get my cane, Mary Ann Marie get me some tapioca pudding." She's only got a limited amount of teeth left in her head – five is what the last count was, so everything has to be soft and runny for her to swallow it. Ma's got a case of the Blues again, so she's taken to staring at the empty space between the couch and the wall – remembering a time before Daddy died I figure. But on the sunny side, I've recently met someone Em. His name is Franklin Harding. He's one of the night shift operators at the plant.

EMILY:

That is such wonderful news. Tell me about him Mary.

MARY:

The first time we met I stared at him for a good twenty minutes before I got past the size of his ears. They are gigantic, and lined throughout in an intricate web of pink veins.

EMILY:

Oh dear…

MARY:

When the sun catches them, those ears twinkle like Christmas tree lights.

EMILY:

Goodness…

MARY:

However he's oddly handsome despite his Dumbo-like appendages. He's come to call on me at the House of Happy once or twice and he always brings Ma and Prune-face chocolates and lollypops. I must admit it makes me positively ill to see that old lady lick those suckers, but at least it shuts her up for a little while. Franklin is enchanting Em. When he looks at me he says my eyes sparkle like the sun. And when he holds my hand he says something about my skin being as soft as a baby's backside. He's not nearly the poet that you are dear Emily, but he's charming in an awkward sort of way.

EMILY:

He sounds very pleasant Mary.

*   *   *

THELMA:

Dear Mary. The Ladies of The Church auxiliary are sponsoring a raffle for the widows of fallen soldiers. Lilly McCormick lost Richard over there and the poor thing doesn't have enough money to buy her groceries. She's such a nervous little thing. I don't see how she will make it without Richard. The point of my letter Mary, is that every little bit counts. I was hoping that you might buy a raffle ticket.

MARY:

Thelma Bernice Rikowski, you can stick that raffle ticket where the sun doesn't shine. I work two miserable jobs just to be able to feed Ma and Prune-face. Don't you be telling me Lilly McCormick's sad stories. She pulled my hair when we were eight and told me I smelled. I'm very sorry that she has fallen on hard times but I will not be buying one of your raffle tickets. Lilly McCormick can take care of herself.

THELMA:

Well I have never heard such an un-Christian response in my entire life. You should be ashamed of yourself. A simple act of charity would do you good Mary Ann. I'm afraid the world has made you a very bitter woman. May God forgive you...

MARY:

I didn't see you having a raffle for my mother after my father died. So while you sit there with your damn church ladies and make lists of all the people that need handouts why don't you take a moment to remember that there is pain everywhere you look my dear Thelma. Whether it's on a beach in France or in your own rotten little town, it's there. And you selling some lousy raffle tickets is nothing but a way to make yourself feel better...

EMILY:

Dear Mary. What did you say to Thelma that has gotten her so sore at you? Mary, she is really quite distressed. And being so worked

up is not good for the baby. Did she tell you
that she's pregnant?

MARY:

Oh for crying out loud, how many babies does
someone need?

EMILY:

Mary Ann Marie, you take that back...

MARY:

That last one is still tottering around in his
didy...

EMILY:

Mary Ann...

MARY:

Thelma is getting married! Thelma is having a
baby! Did you hear? Thelma's having another
baby!

EMILY:

Mary stop...

MARY:

By golly Thelma is back in the family way
again! I'm tired of blowing my wig for Thelma.

*   *   *

THELMA:

Dear Emily. The Ladies of The Church auxiliary would like to thank you for buying a raffle ticket. Your donation has gone to help those widows and children in need. God bless you for your kindness and generosity.

*   *   *

EMILY:

Dear Mary. This is such exciting news about you and Franklin Harding. How did he ask you? Did he drop to one knee? Did he talk about your skin and your eyes? Did he say he wanted to make you the happiest woman on earth?

MARY:

No, I told him it was time to make an honest woman of me and he said, "Well okie-dokie then, I guess I had better marry you."

EMILY:

Oh, well, that's nice, isn't it?

MARY:

Ma is a new woman. The news seems to have cured her Blues. Even Old Prune-face is smiling with that toothless mouth of hers. Have I mentioned that those last three teeth are about to fall out from sucking on all of those lollypops that Franklin supplies her with?

EMILY:

I told Thelma the great news.

MARY:

What did she say?

EMILY:

She said she hopes that you will be very happy.

*   *   *

MARY:

Dear Emily. Ma says it is necessary to celebrate these things. She says weddings are a rite of passage. I say phooey, but if it puts a smile on the woman's face I figure it's the least I could do. She bought me a dress Em, with lace and little bows and stuff on it. I don't know how I will ever keep a straight face wearing that frilly thing. But I love Franklin Harding Em. I love him. I hope that you and Thelma will be here. You will be here, won't you Em?

EMILY:

I would not miss it for all the angels in heaven.

*   *   *

MARY:

Dear Thelma. Let me start by saying congratulations on your pregnancy. I knew when I saw you holding the baby Jesus in the pageant all those years ago that you were born to be a mother. You're a good mother Thelma – and a good Christian woman. Thelma I'm sorry. I'm sorry for the things that I said to you. You're thoughtful in so many ways that I am not. I hope that you can accept my apology and be a part of my wedding day.

THELMA:

Your apology is accepted Mary. And yes…

EMILY:

We'll see you next week Mary…

THELMA:

Of course I will be a part of your wedding day. I love you to pieces Mary Ann…

EMILY:

Will you be at the train to meet us Mary?

MARY:

Stop. Don't come.

*   *   *

THELMA:

Dear Mary. That Franklin is a simply despicable man. Any person that is capable of such evil behavior is not a man that any woman should marry. I know that things have not been good between us recently, but I want you to know that I never stopped loving you for even one little minute. You and Emily are my oldest and dearest friends in this world. You are both family to me. Please know that you are always in my prayers. God never gives us more than we can handle. He knew that you, with all of your fortitude and good humor could handle this heartache. With the Lord's guidance, you will pull through this. Love, Thelma

EMILY:

Mary, I'm sorry that it has taken me so long to write. I have been trying to think of the words to say to you. Franklin Harding is a very, very bad person for doing what he did. Whoever that Loretta is, she could not be half as wonderful as you are. Life isn't very kind sometimes is it Mary?

* * *

MARY:

Dear Emily. Prune-face is a diabetic. If it had not been for her unquenchable thirst and her hollering in the middle of the night that she needs help getting to the toilet, we would never have known that the old bat's insulin levels are out of whack. Guess who gets to stick her insulin shots in that saggy waddle on the back of her arm? Why little ol' me.

THELMA:

Dear Mary. Emily told me about your grandmother. Are you okay dear?

EMILY:

Mary, why don't you come for a visit? Get away for a while...

THELMA:

Yes, Mary why don't you...

MARY:

Get away? Why on earth would I want to do that ya'll? I'm having way too much fun here at the House of Happy.

EMILY:

Thelma and I are worried about you Mar…

THELMA:

Have you heard from Franklin?

EMILY:

Mary, have you given our invitation some more thought? I think it would be good if you came for a visit. I mean after what happened with…

MARY:

Stop feeling sorry for me ya'll. I'm fine. Just stop. I don't want to talk about this ever again. I've got to go now. Prune-face needs her shot. (cont'd)

*   *   *

MARY:

Dear Thelma. Congratulations on the birth of Rita…

THELMA:

Thank you Mary. We are truly…

MARY:

I know how happy you and George must…

THELMA:

Yes, indeed the Lord has blessed us again with…

MARY:

Dear Emily. Help! Ma's playing matchmaker. She says there isn't much time left to find me a husband. Apparently my sole purpose in life is to make proper use of my eggs. Ma says I'm going to wake up one day not too long from now and be an old maid with shrived up eggs. Yesterday she invited our neighbor's grandson over for coffee – claimed he was coming over to sell us a new bible. But when I asked him about his bibles he cocked his head to the side and shrugged his shoulders and said, "Excuse me? I'm afraid I don't got any bibles to sell you lady." To which Ma says, "You don't need no bible Mary. You already got a bible. What you need is a nice fella."

EMILY:

Oh no…

MARY:

Then she says, "Do you think my Mary's pretty Larry?"

EMILY:

She said that?

MARY:

Em, he's no taller than a twelve-year-old girl. He's got dwarfed limbs and a lisp. He looks me up and down and says, "Well yes ma'am I suppose she's pretty enough." And then out of no where he blurts, "Ma'am I'm a sinner. I've been in the state pen. I robbed two liquor stores on my eighteenth birthday." And then Ma says, "Let bygones be bygones young man and you take my Mary to the picture show." Apparently Em, it's better to be married to a criminal than no one at all.

*   *   *

THELMA:

Dearest family and friends. May God fill your life with love, joy and peace this holiday season and throughout the New Year. Love, the Rikowski family

EMILY:

Merry Christmas Mary. Is it true? Thelma told me that you went on a date with Larry?

MARY:

Yes, but Thelma is under the impression that he's a graduate of Penn State and sells bibles for a living. I know – I couldn't help myself.

*　　*　　*

EMILY:

Dear Mary. Guess what? I met a nice gentleman by the name of Warren Templeton. He sells knives and garden tools and various other instruments out of the back of his Buick Estate Wagon. He was only in Lark Eden for the night on his way up to Charleston. He came into the Texaco to buy a pack of Pall Malls and when I was ringing him up he asked me if he could take me out for a steak dinner. It wasn't forward like it sounds Mar. He was a perfect gentleman. I told him my shift wasn't over until 9:30 and it would be too late to eat steaks. He said he would wait all night if he had to, just to have dinner with a pretty lady like myself. Turns out it was too late to eat dinner at a restaurant. So we just walked and talked. Then he drove me home and told me that he would be back through Lark Eden on his way home from Charleston. He kept saying that he wanted to treat me to a nice steak dinner. He's very pleasant Mary.

MARY:

Careful Em, you don't know a thing about him. For all you know he takes women out for steak dinners in every town across the South and hacks them up into little bitsy pieces with the knives in the back of the Buick Estate Wagon. (cont'd)

* * *

MARY:

Dear Thelma. Prune-face is going to lose her foot, maybe the whole leg. The Doc says he's got to lop if off. She stepped on a loose floorboard and a nail went right through her big toe. You should have seen it – this big purple foot with a nail sticking out of that crusty old toe. It was enough to make me sick. It got infected and now she's going to lose the foot. Ma can't stop crying – says she's tired of the constant disappointment and sad news. Every time there is the least little bit of bad news around here she starts wailing about my eggs. Says I better marry Larry and have a few babies before it's too late.

THELMA:

Your grandmother is in my prayers Mary.

MARY:

Lost the leg from the knee down. She spent five nights at St. Vincent's Hospital after the operation and now she's back home sweet home at the House of Happy. Now whenever I walk by her bedroom, all I see is her stump flopping around on the bed. You'd think the least they could have done was made a clean slice and sewn it up pretty, but it looks like someone took a cleaver to it. Speaking of, how's Emily's knife salesman?

THELMA:

He's called her on the telephone every day since he came back through town two months ago. I think our little Emily is in love with the salesman. Maybe you and Em will both marry your salesman! You see Mary I told you that God has a plan for us!

MARY:

Careful Thel. Don't blow your wig.

* * *

EMILY:

Dear Mary. Warren proposed to me! He took me out for a steak dinner and after he paid the bill he looked at me all moony and said, "Let's you a me get married Puss." Can you believe it Mary, I'm twenty-eight years old and I'm getting married? I guess it's never too late old friend. The only sad part is I will be moving to Florida, which makes the distance between us even farther. I can hardly bear the thought of being so far from you and Thelma. But I figure I haven't seen you since Paul was born, and we still manage to write these letters, and somehow I feel that you are never far from my heart.

*   *   *

MARY:

Dear Emily. It was a beautiful wedding. You looked beautiful. And happy – you looked happy Em.

THELMA:

Mary, it was wonderful to see you at Emily's wedding. It was almost as if no time has passed. It is remarkable when you think about it, that we have been friends for so many years. Love, Thelma. P.S. I can hardly wait to meet the Bible salesman.

*   *   *

EMILY:

Greetings from Pinellas Park, Florida. Would you believe that I had not been here for even a day when Warren had to leave on another sales trip? I guess I will have to get use to being the wife of a traveling salesman.

THELMA:

Dear Emily. I miss you. I can't believe how different it feels without you here in Lark Eden. Elizabeth, Paul and little Rita miss you too.

*   *   *

EMILY:

Dear Thelma. I've recently taken a job in the deli at the Winn Dixie. Not because we are in desperate need of the money, mind you, but because I'm lonesome when Warren is away and I figured I needed something to keep my mind off my lonesomeness. Other than the hair net that they make me wear, I am enjoying my new job slicing lunchmeat and serving up breaded cutlets. My coworkers are very pleasant. Betty Wippleman, who recently got promoted to cashier, always includes me on her afternoon cigarette breaks. She doesn't seem to mind much that I don't smoke. She can talk the ears off a Billy goat but I enjoy her company. It looks like I might make some new friends!

THELMA:

Horns, talk the horns off a Billy goat. Oh how I love you Miss Emily. I love you to pieces.

*　*　*

MARY:

Dear Emily. Thelma said you called last night crying. I know that you miss Lark Eden Em. Though nothing can bring back those days in our beloved hometown, we will always have the memories. Remember when we were eight and we had a funeral service for that red and yellow butterfly that you accidently ran over with your father's wheelbarrow? Remember how you cried and Thelma asked God to forgive you for your sins? And then remember how I told you that it would all be all right? It will be Em. It will all be all right. I love you. Write soon.

*　*　*

THELMA:

May His love and presence be inside you this joyous Christmas Season. Love the Rikowski Family. P.S. How's the Bible salesman?

MARY:

His love and presence is inside me this joyous...

THELMA:

Don't be crude Mary Ann. Have you heard from Em?

MARY:

Yoo-hoo Emily, are you there?

THELMA:

Emily, where are you? How come you don't return my phone calls?

MARY:

Hello, are you there, Em? I tried to call you last night. Are you all right?

* * *

EMILY:

Dear Mary. I'm having a baby! Imagine Mary, I'm nearly thirty and I'm having a baby. Warren is beside himself with joy. I think he secretly wants a boy. I could care a less if it's a girl or a boy, as long as it's healthy. See you were right – it will all be all right!

MARY:

Well all right then. Isn't that nice.

THELMA:

This is such wonderful news. The Lord works in mysterious ways my dear Emily. Sometimes when we least expect it, our Father in heaven blesses us with the most precious gift of all. (cont'd)

*   *   *

THELMA:

Dear Emily. How are you dear? To be a mother is the most important thing you will ever do in your entire life. Soon you will see Em. May the Lord smile upon you dearest Emily. (cont'd)

*   *   *

THELMA:

Emily? Are you there dear? (cont'd)

*   *   *

THELMA:

Mary, I'm writing to tell you that Emily lost the baby. God rest its soul…

EMILY:

Dear Mary. When God took from me the one thing in this world that would make me happy, that would make it all right, I knew that I was done believing in things…

THELMA:

Pray Mary. Please pray that God will give our Emily the strength that she needs to…

EMILY:

You said it would be all right, you promised Mary. Life isn't very kind is it?

THELMA:

I'm headed down to Florida the day after tomorrow to be with her…

MARY:

Does she know you're coming?

THELMA:

No, I'm just going. P.S. I'm pregnant, but please don't tell Emily, not yet anyway.

EMILY:

Mary, enclosed is a poem that I wrote last night:

A mother weeps for a child that she will never know.
The light above casts its long black shadows on her,
and in her dream there is a butterfly that takes flight.
And then the child comes to her.
She rocks her child under a flicker of red and yellow wings,
and then she wakes and the nightmare takes flight.
And then the mother dies.

MARY:

Thelma, I'm getting on the next bus to Pinellas Park. P.S. Larry and I broke it off. And he's not a bible salesman. And he didn't go to Penn State. He went to the state pen.

ACT TWO

EMILY:

Dear Thelma. Happy first birthday to the twins! Please give those little angels big kisses for me. One of these days I'll get to see my godchildren.

THELMA:

Em, I love you to pieces. Emily May and Jean are blessed to have a godmother as special as you are my dear Em.

MARY:

Dear Emily. I tried to call last night but Warren said you had a headache and couldn't come to the phone. Is everything all right?

EMILY:

You don't need to worry that I'm going to kill myself old friend. Since you and Thelma kindly kept your vigil by my bedside, time is slowly healing my wounds. Writing helps, whether it's letters to you and Thelma or poems, I somehow feel better when I get it out, still sad but a better kind of sad. I worry about Warren though. He's distant somehow. He won't say it, but I just know that he wants a child. I feel like I've failed by not being able to give him one.

MARY:

Em, you have not failed. Besides, I think Thelma has enough children for all of us. Keep writing Emily. (cont'd)

* * *

MARY:

Dear Thelma. It's official. Prune-face lost her last remaining tooth. Ma insisted that she be fitted with a set of dentures. They are these marvelous shiny plates of big perfect teeth. Problem is, she says they hurt her gums. So I imagine they will spend more time in the empty prune juice glass next to her bed than in her mouth.

* * *

THELMA:

Dear Mary. My Elizabeth is getting married to Will Stark. She's pregnant.

MARY:

Jesus Thelma, she's just a kid. How did this happen?

THELMA:

Well my dear Mary let me give you a lesson on
the birds and...

MARY:

Does she love Will Stark?

THELMA:

That is beside the point. She's having a baby
and Will Stark will be a good father to that
little baby. He's good at just about everything
he touches. He's the smartest boy in his senior
class, the captain of the football team and he is
the best boy in the whole school at...

MARY:

Getting sixteen year old girls in the family
way?

THELMA:

You should be ashamed of yourself Mary for
being so crude at a time like this. He will be a
wonderful father to that little baby. And
besides, I can hardly wait to be a...

EMILY:

My goodness Thel, a grandmother at the ripe
old age of thirty-five.

THELMA:

Laura is a beautiful baby Em. She looks just like Liz did when she was born. Will took a job in West Virginia with a plastics manufacturer. He was going to start college in the fall but he says he wants to be responsible and provide for his family. Of course Mary said he should go to college anyway. But what does our Mary know about marriage...

MARY:

Dear Emily. I've taken a lover...

THELMA:

What does Mary know about the responsibilities of family?

MARY:

His name is Edward and he teaches English at the public high school. He is marvelously handsome in a rugged sort of way. There is one small problem. He's married. Please don't tell Thelma. She would scold me for my sins.

* * *

THELMA:

Dear Mary. May Jesus always be your joy, your hope, your song. And may this Christmas and each day of the New Year be directed by His guided hand of love. Love, The Rikowski Family

MARY:

Dear Emily. Edward is my joy, my hope, my song. And this Christmas and each day of the New Year will be directed by his guided hand of love. Please, not a word to Thelma.

*   *   *

EMILY:

Dear Thelma. I'm writing because I can't hold it in any longer. I need to tell someone. Warren hasn't sold any knives in nearly six months and he is getting more and more despondent. He says he's failed me in so many ways. He prattles on about how he is unable to give me a child and unable to provide for me in the proper way. I tell him that I don't need fancy things and that I don't even need a child to be happy – just him. It's funny, I thought that I had let him down, but it turns out he thinks he's the one doing the disappointing.

THELMA:

My dearest Emily. I am so sorry to hear about your troubles. Men are peculiar creatures indeed. It's hard to figure them sometimes. Just give it time and I'm sure that Warren will feel better. Remember Em, God works in...

EMILY:

I'm terribly worried about his behavior. He wears the same white t-shirts day after day – ones that go yellow at the underarms and expose curly sprouts of hair poking out of their v-shaped neck holes. He drinks malt liquor beverages on the back porch and smokes his Pall Malls down to the nubbin. He even drinks in the morning hours.

THELMA:

God has a plan for us. I know that sometimes it's hard to see the way when these hard times befall us, but in time you will see that your husband will come back to you just like my husband came home to me all those years ago...

MARY:

Hi-di-ho from the beaches of North Carolina. Edward told his wife some story about having to go to Charlotte to visit his sister. So here we are having a romantic weekend on the shore...

EMILY:

Dear Thelma. Yesterday at breakfast Warren started to sob in his Cream of Wheat. He kept saying, "I'm sorry Puss, I'm sorry Puss." He said it over and over and then he confessed that he has been unfaithful to me. He met a young woman in Jacksonville on one of his sales trips. He said it was years ago, right after we were married. Apparently he took this woman out for steak dinners whenever he came through town...

MARY:

Em, the place we're staying is a marvelous little motel on the beach...

THELMA:

Emily, you listen to me dear. Sometimes these things happen, men can't help themselves. It's the way that God made them. Sometimes the temptations overcome them and these things just happen...

EMILY:

Please don't tell Mary...

THELMA:

Not a word...

MARY:

We can see the sunsets and hear the waves crashing from our room. I have to go now. Edward wants more of me. He cannot seem to get enough of me! I'm coming darling. Life is grand, isn't it Em? Abyssinia!

*   *   *

EMILY:

Life's not very kind is it Thelma? I may not be terribly smart and educated but I know that we should stay out of this war. I can't stop thinking about how George's cousin Paul died on that beach in France so many years ago. That image of him dying on that beach always comes swimming back to me when I least expect it.

*   *   *

MARY:

Back at the House of Happy with Ma and Prune-face.

*   *   *

EMILY:

Happy birthday Mary. How does it feel on the
other side of the hill?

MARY:

If this is what over the hill feels like, I feel
better than I ever have in my life. I've got to go
now. Edward is waiting for me in the car and
Prune-face just gave me a gummy smirk and
started in with the questions.

*   *   *

EMILY:

Dear Mary. What is the world coming to, I ask
you? When a single bullet rings out into the
day and kills our president riding in a car, I
feel that there is not much left that we can
count on in this world.

*   *   *

MARY:

Dear Emily. When Edward picked me up a few
nights ago he was crying – all red-faced and
blubbering. When he finally calmed down, he
informed me that he left his wife for me. Shit
Em, shit. If you could have seen him crying
like he was. His face Em, I can't get it out of my

mind. It hadn't been an hour and he was already missing her. I'm a horrible, horrible person. Remember when we were fifteen and I kissed Sammy Wiener even though I knew you loved him? Em, I am still the same rotten person. I don't know what it is that causes me to act this way. I can't believe that I have caused this woman pain. That poor woman, I can't imagine how terrible she must feel knowing that her husband was unfaithful. I should be punished for my sins.

EMILY:

Maybe you should tell Thelma.

MARY:

No, never! Promise me you will never tell her what I have done. Promise?

EMILY:

I promise Mary.

*   *   *

THELMA:

Dear Mary. Paul is being deployed to Vietnam within the week. Pray for my boy Mary. Do you promise that you'll pray?

MARY:

I promise Thelma.

*   *   *

EMILY:

Dear Mary. I'm writing to tell you that Warren and I are moving to the trailer park down the road. No need to get alarmed, but about a week ago Warren fell asleep on the couch with a cigarette lit. He's all right, thank goodness, but the damage to the house we're renting is extensive. Had it not been for little old Mrs. Wong stopping by to return the garden tools that she borrowed I'm afraid the whole house would have burned up. When I got home from work there were two fire trucks in front of the house and they had Warren in the back of an ambulance. He suffered from smoke inhalation. And Mrs. Wong suffered heat stroke from running back to her house to call 911. Our new address is 235 US 19 N. Pinellas Park, FL 33781. I guess it's a good thing I've been working all those extra shifts at the Winn Dixie. We used all the money to buy the trailer and the rest we got from Warren's aunt in Tallahassee. It's only twenty by sixty feet, but nonetheless it's a place to call home. I plan on planting a vegetable garden and Warren said he's going to build a picnic table out back. He says it'll be like having a whole other room outdoors.

MARY:

Your trailer sounds awful Em. I don't know what's worse being stuck in a house with wheels or being stuck with Ma and Prune-face in the House of Happy.

EMILY:

It's not so bad – less to clean. Have you heard from Edward?

MARY:

No, not since I told him we could never see each other again. I told him to go home to his wife. And Em, I don't ever want to talk about him again.

*   *   *

THELMA:

Dear Emily. I'm writing this from the hospital. George has been having horrible headaches for the last couple of months. At first I thought it must be from the stress at the plant and the worry about Paul in Vietnam. To be honest, I didn't pay much attention to his groaning about the pain until last night when he woke me up in the middle of the night and told me he needed to go to the hospital because the pain was excruciating. They're taking good care of him here. He's having more tests this afternoon. I'm sure it's nothing a little rest won't cure. I'll write when I know more. Please call Mary and tell her not to worry.

*   *   *

EMILY:

Dear Mary. Seeing you last week made me miss you all the more old friend. I only wish that we could have seen each other under happier circumstances. Our Thelma is the strongest woman I have ever known. The way she sat there in that pew between the twins and held their hands, and the way she had everyone back to the house after the service for sandwiches and coffee. Her faith and her love for her children are so strong. I'm rather envious of her Mar. Even though she has lost her husband she has so much that I will never know. Sure I have Warren, but he's not very good company these days. I'm alone in this world Mary. And I've stopped believing in things. When I was a little girl I would get sad, but somehow I always believed. Believed in tomorrow, believed in possibilities, believed in what's coming next. And now every time I start believing, something terrible happens. At George's funeral I just sat there in that church and listened to the drone of the organ and stared straight ahead at those shiny Jesus toes that I stared at so many years ago at your father's funeral. And it was at that moment that I realized that I'm still the same sad little girl that I was at sixteen. Only difference is I don't believe any more.

MARY:

My dear sweet Emily. Believe, believe, believe! You have to try Em, because without it life ain't worth a damn if you ask me. And yes our Thelma is a strong old broad, but don't you fool yourself, she's terrified of what's coming next. You can believe in God all you want, but let's face it God ain't going to pay the bills. And those twins don't look right if you ask me – just a couple of pimply potheads. They looked as high as a Georgia pine. And what happened to little Rita? The rear end on that girl is tremendous. She must weigh 300 pounds. And that Paul acts like he got some shrapnel lodged in his brain over there. He acted like he was at a brothel rather than his father's funeral. How many beers can one possibly guzzle in the course of two hours? What's wrong with him Em? He doesn't have the sense that God gave a gopher – sitting there after the service scratching his belly with that smile glued stupidly on his face. I don't care what war you've been fighting in. What I'm trying to say Em is Thelma has a long road ahead of her. Sure she'll pull through this, but she doesn't have it as easy as it looks. And Emily, you are not alone. You have me. And as for me, I have Ma and Prune-face. So from the House of Happy to my trailer trash friend in Florida, goodbye for now. Love, Mary P.S. Get back to your poetry.

*   *   *

THELMA:

Dear Mary. I am sorry to hear that your grandmother is slipping. You've been good to her over the years Mar. God sees your goodness. Thank you for calling me on the anniversary of George's death. It's hard to believe that it's been a year since my beloved husband entered the gates of heaven. God bless you old friend.

*   *   *

MARY:

Dear Thelma. Last night just before the clock stuck twelve, Old Prune-face hobbled on her one and only leg past the pearly gates. I can only hope that George was there to greet her. I know that I said some spiteful things about that woman over the years. God knows she was just an old stump of a woman. Just a nasty, purple old lady with one leg and no teeth by the time it was all said and done. Squawking and hollering until she gasped her last breathe. Truth be told, all her discontent and that purple, squashed face of hers was something I came to count on. Love is a strange thing, isn't it Thelma? Sometimes we don't even know we're doing it until it's too late. I never told the old bat that I loved her – not once. And just between you and me, I regret it. I just thought I would share my come to Jesus moment with the one person who I knew would appreciate it.

*   *   *

THELMA:

May His love surround you and bring you a most joyous Christmas Season. Love, Thelma

MARY:

Thel, Emily wrote and said that you're going to spend Christmas with Liz and Will and the girls. Please give my love to everyone.

EMILY:

Merry Christmas from Tallahassee. Warren and I are spending Christmas with his aunt.

MARY:

Hello from the House of Happy! Yes another Christmas has come and gone and Ma's still bitching and complaining. And when she does shut up it's only because she's been snatched by another case of the Blues.

* * *

EMILY:

Dear Thelma. I was thinking maybe you and Mary could come for a visit. When was the last time that we all got together when it didn't have to do with a wedding or a christening or a funeral? I think the last time may have been when you and Mar came to my rescue after I had the miscarriage, and that certainly wasn't a bucket of laughs now was it? What do you think Thelma?

THELMA:

I think it's a great idea Em. What does Mary say?

MARY:

I'd love to Emily. How's March? Thelma's fiftieth is at the end of the month. We could celebrate in style – just some old dames kicking back on the beach sipping Rum Runners and Mai Tais.

THELMA:

Old? Who are you calling old? I don't feel any different that I did when we were fifteen.

EMILY:

Warren has a cousin who can get us a discount at some motel on the beach in Clearwater. It won't be luxurious but it's better than all piling into the trailer, right Mar?

THELMA:

I booked my flight to Tampa. I get in at 2:15 in the afternoon. I think I'm almost as excited about getting on an airplane for the first time in my life as I am about seeing my old friends.

MARY:

See ya'll in a few days!

EMILY:

Even Warren thinks it will be good for me to see "your girls" as he calls you.

THELMA:

Something has come up. I can't make it.

*   *   *

MARY:

Dear Thelma. I've been trying to call you for a week. Jean keeps answering the phone and telling me that you're not home or that you're sleeping. Sleeping? Since when do you sleep at noon? You've never taken a nap in your life. What's going on?

THELMA:

Dear Mary. I'm sorry that I haven't written or called. It's been a difficult couple of weeks for our family. The important thing is that we are a family and that we have each other. Pray that God will watch over us during this trying time.

MARY:

Jesus H. Christ Thelma. What is all this bullshit about *your* family? Emily and I are your family too. And we deserve to know what's going on. All this holier than thou crap is not going to cut it this time my friend. What is going on?

THELMA:

Mary, I would appreciate it if you could refrain from taking the Lord's name in vain. And if you insist on knowing my private family matters, here it is: Paul has been arrested for homicide by vehicle.

MARY:

Oh Thel…

THELMA:

But my dear boy didn't mean to do it. He's innocent Mary. He was doing what men do after work, drinking. He was having a couple of beers at McGee's after his shift at the plant and it appears that he was intoxicated when he got in his car. And he hit someone, a child. He killed him. It was Lilly Burns' grandson. Do you remember Lilly McCormick? You so kindly refused to make a charitable donation after Richard died in the war. Well she remarried Randal Burns and she had two children and then she had two grandchildren. And now God rest his soul, one of those little boys is…

MARY:

Jesus Thelma…

THELMA:

God have mercy on my Paul...

MARY:

That's the most terrible thing I have ever heard. What can I do to help? Do you want me to come there?

THELMA:

No. Stay away Mary. Please don't come. I'll call if I need anything.

*   *   *

EMILY:

Dear Mary. The lawyer that Thelma hired is trying to get Paul's sentence reduced due to the fact that the psychiatrist said he was suffering from post-traumatic stress disorder from fighting in Vietnam. He claims that his reckless behavior is a result of having to fight in that awful war. That war is responsible for this Mary...

MARY:

How's Thelma?

EMILY:

She sounded good when I talked to her yesterday. I think she's spending every last cent of George's pension on legal fees. Poor Paul, he didn't even need to say it, I could just tell by looking at him the last time we saw him – I saw it in his eyes. Mary he died in that war. There is so much pain in what folks don't speak of.

THELMA:

Pray for my boy. He will need your prayers when they take him away to jail.

MARY:

I will Thelma.

*   *   *

MARY:

Greetings from The House of Happy. How's trailer park life Em? Life here is grand. Ma's even more miserable since Prune-face kicked it. She got some doctor to give her little pink happy pills – suppose to cure her Blues I guess. I think she just needs some fresh air and to stop with the self-pity act. Who ever heard of such a thing? Pills to make you happy? She says the reason she's so damn miserable is that

I never gave her any grandchildren. Says she never got the chance to be a grandmother. Grandmother? I say phooey – she couldn't even be a proper mother for Christ sake. What makes her think she would get it right this time?

EMILY:

I would love to get my hands on those little pink pills. Everything makes me sad these days. I can't even look at Warren anymore without feeling sad. When we met he was so full of passion and life, and now all that he seems to care about are situation comedies. He just sits in the muffle of canned laughter coming off the television and smokes one Pall Mall after another. The only time he gets out of his chair is to change the channel and move the aluminum foil around on the TV antennas. And to top it all off Mar – I'm getting fat.

MARY:

Fat, I don't believe it.

EMILY:

Believe it Mary – believe it. On the TV people that are in love are thin and watery-eyed and touch each other's faces when they smooch. In real life love just makes me sad.

*   *   *

THELMA:

Dear Mary. Rejoice in His blessings and may His love be with you during this Christmas Season. Love Thelma

MARY:

Dear Thelma, how are you…

THELMA:

Wishing your Easter is decorated with love, peace, and joys of Spring and God's Blessings!

MARY:

Well Thel there sure ain't no peace and joy around the House of Happy. Ma's taken to fiercely clipping articles from *The National Inquirer* about people who smashed head first into rock bottom before they found the strength they never knew they had. Charming little tales of drug addicts and prostate cancer patients and schizophrenics who opt not to stick their head in the oven but instead start a cat rescue. It's as if Ma's trying to console herself with other people's woes. The clippings keep showing up in my bedroom. I caught her skulking around in my room a couple of days ago. "Oh Mary you startled me," she said lurching forth with a fistful of crumpled clippings. "I just wanted to leave you this article about a midget born without feet who swam the English Channel to raise money for Alzheimer's disease."

THELMA:

May your heart and home be filled with the true spirit of Jesus this Christmas. Love, Thelma

MARY:

Thel, How are you old friend? How's Paul doing? How are the twins? Emily told me that Jean moved to Savannah? You must miss her. How's Rita? Has she lost any of that weight? She is such a pretty girl. It's a shame that she's such a Two-Ton Tilly. Once she sheds some of those pounds she will have to watch out, the fellas are not going to know what hit them. Please give my love to the whole family Thel. I love you old girl.

THELMA:

Easter blessings for all my dear friends and family.

*   *   *

EMILY:

Merry Christmas and Happy New Year to you Mary. Enclosed is a picture that Warren took of me with Clark Gable. He's the puppy that I was telling you about that we adopted from that sweet little black boy who had a box of pups in front of K-mart. It was that darn syringe that the kid was feeding those pups with that got me Mar. They were all aiming for that thing like it was their mamma's nipple. That big fake nipple made me all warm inside. Love Emily, Warren and Clark Gable

MARY:

Em, you're right, you have gotten fat. Merry Christmas.

*   *   *

EMILY:

Dear Mary. Thelma called last night. Paul gets out next week. I guess Thelma's planning a big special homecoming for him.

MARY:

For crying out loud, the poor guy just lost nearly eight years of his life locked up in an eight-foot cell. He might not be up for celebrating.

THELMA:

My Paul's home Mary! And he looks fabulous.

*   *   *

EMILY:

Dear Mary. Clark Gable has recently developed the habit of howling at sirens. He sits outside next to the picnic table and yowls like he's calling out to his beloved. Like he's filled with mournfulness.

MARY:

He and Ma should get together sometime. I can just see it, Ma and old Clark Gable letting loose some long sad howls.

*   *   *

THELMA:

Merry Christmas to all of our cherished family and friends. Our family has been so blessed by the Lord this past year. Liz and Will and the girls moved to Beckley where Will is working for West Virginia Engineering Plastics in the sales division. He's been with the company for almost twenty-five years and still loving it. We are all so proud of our new graduate! After many late nights studying while working a full time job, my oldest granddaughter Laura graduated with a degree in French Literature from West Virginia University. As for Will and Liz's youngest girls, well it's hard to believe that those beautiful little babies are going to be thirteen and fourteen next year. Time does fly. My twins are both living in Savannah. We all knew that it would only be a matter of time before Emily May would follow Jean there. And the most exciting news is that Jean is having another baby! She's due at the end of March. We have all been so happy to have Paul home. It's been almost one full year and his strong faith and regular Bible Study have given him a new lease on life. We hope that God has blessed you as much as He has blessed us this year. From all of us to you: Merry Christmas and a very healthy and Happy New Year! Love, The Rikowskis

MARY:

Dear Emily. Did you get that nauseating Christmas card from Thelma? I'll tell you, she is so full of hot air. Bible Study, give me a break. Poor Paul needs a lot more help than he can get from reading the Bible. She failed to mention that he's in AA. But then again Thelma thought that AA was the Automobile Association of America. And your namesake

Emily May moved in with her sister because her manic depression is so bad that Thelma begged Jean to take her in to be on suicide watch. And there was absolutely no mention of that poor fatty Rita. It's like she doesn't exist.

EMILY:

Actually it was me who thought that AA was the Automobile Association of America.

*   *   *

THELMA:

Dear Mary. Emily and I both think that you should think about putting your mother in a nursing home. I got the names of some wonderful places near Huntsville from one of the ladies in the auxiliary. She said Sunnybrook Acres is a lovely place. Here's a brochure. Look how everyone is smiling. It looks like a super place.

MARY:

Dearest Thelma. The reason that everyone is smiling is because the old farts can't hear a word that anyone is saying to them. Look at them all happily drooling into their little plastic tubs of canned peaches. Sunnybrook Acres – where did they get a name like that? Acres? It's one lousy building where the staff is grossly underpaid and the halls smell like industrial-strength soup. I swear the names of those places are a hoot – ol' Sunnybrook Acres.

THELMA:

We just think that you have your hands full taking care of your mother. She might need the kind of care that you're unable to give her. She might be happier at Sunnybrook.

MARY:

I appreciate the concern Thelma, but I'm not putting my mother in a nursing home. Those places smell like soup. I can manage.

*   *   *

EMILY:

Mary, enclosed is a picture of Clark Gable on his birthday. I made him a cake out of hamburger meat and wrote a poem for him. I think he liked the cake more than the poem. I love that little guy so much. Here's the poem:

Broken down to my knees
Unable to accept the saddest things in life
Never fully understanding the ache
I waited for something to believe in.
And then with a warm kiss and a lone bark
From a box writhing with life

You made me believe.

*   *   *

MARY:

Dear Thelma. Being old sure ain't no fun is it? One of my best attributes, hands down, was my eyebrows. For most of my life complete strangers paid me compliments on my perfectly groomed arcs. Now I'm lucky if I can find nine hairs to comb into place. They just stopped growing.

THELMA:

Oh honey, all the hair that once grew out of the places that the good Lord intended it to grow is now growing out of my chin.

MARY:

Why Miss Thelma Bernice, I do believe that you just cracked a joke.

*   *   *

THELMA:

Dear Mary. Last night Emily and I both had a few too many glasses of Chablis while we were gabbing on the telephone and we came up with the craziest idea. How about if we girls take a trip somewhere together? I want to fly on an airplane to someplace exotic. How does Buffalo sound? Will's boss has a house on Lake Erie that is only used in the summer months. Liz said we would be welcome to use it in the fall.

MARY:

I can't go. Who will I get to take care of Ma? Someone has to give the old bat her meds. Guess what, she's got gout.

THELMA:

Mary, here's the telephone number of an agency that you can hire to look after your mother for the week.

EMILY:

It's a bit pricey.

THELMA:

But Emily and I are going to help pay for it. We insist Mary Ann Marie.

EMILY:

Five days till we are all together again!

THELMA:

Who would have thought, a bunch of old southern ladies whooping it up in Buffalo!

MARY:

I can hardly wait to see you both! Hang on – Ma's calling me. I'm back. I had to give her her pills. I should have given her cyanide.

THELMA:

I can hardly wait to fly on that airplane!

MARY:

Abyssinia!

EMILY:

I can't go. I'm sorry. But I can't go. (cont'd)

*   *   *

EMILY:

Dear Mary. Thank you for coming after Clark Gable died. That dog was the reason that I got out of bed in the morning Mary. I know that it sounds silly, because he was just an old dog, but that furry guy made me so happy. Warren and I buried his ashes under the picnic table because that's where he always sat and howled at the sirens. I don't know if Thelma understands like you do Mary. I think she thought I was a crazy old woman for not going on our trip to Buffalo because my dog died.

THELMA:

Dearest Emily. I came across this poem that I thought would be of some comfort to you. The author is unknown. I substituted the name Clark Gable for the name in the poem.

Heaven is where all of the dogs
That I have ever loved will come running to greet me.
Clark Gable my beloved Earth Angel
Will be leading the pack

EMILY:

Thank you Thelma. Thank you.

* * *

THELMA:

Dear Mary. Do you think Emily will be all right?

MARY:

She'll be all right.

*   *   *

EMILY:

Happy birthday Mary! How does it feel to be that old?

MARY:

You're only as old as you feel Em. How is it that I'm one hundred and twenty-five years old already?

*   *   *

EMILY:

Dear Mary. I have some wonderful news about our dear Thelma...

MARY:

Thelma, why didn't you tell me that Elmer Carmichael was courting you? I can't believe you haven't mentioned it. Tell me all of the details please. Pretty please...

THELMA:

Carol only died six months ago, God rest her soul. Elmer told me that he has only loved two women in his life – Carol and me. But he says he loved me first. I'm not sure I believe the part about loving me first, we were just kids for goodness sake. And yes he is courting me Mary Ann. He is talking about wanting to marry me. I am way too old for all of this nonsense. I've been a widow for nearly forty years. And I'll tell you one thing I am not about to share my bed with Elmer Carmichael now.

MARY:

Why Miss Thelma are you blushing over there?

THELMA:

Mary Ann Marie don't you start with...

MARY:

Has he tried to kiss you?

THELMA:

Now you leave me alone.

*   *   *

EMILY:

I've never believed in angels or heaven, or a fiery hell for that matter. I try Mary. I try to believe it. But no one seems to have any hard evidence of anything beyond what we know is right here. They say you see your life race back and forth across your eyes and then you see angels with gossamer wings sputtering in a hazy light and then you slip away. But it seems to me the only ones who might have access to this kind of information would be the dead ones. So, my question is, how do we know any of this if these poor souls are strolling around with the dead folks in heaven. I mean honestly Mary, how am I supposed to believe what a bunch of dead people have to say?

MARY:

You are a funny old lady. Are you mustering up all these ghoulish thoughts because Thelma told you Lilly Burns died? Miss Lilly, God rest her soul, has quite literally had one foot in the grave for almost ten years. That body of hers quit a long time ago. Not to mention that dementia snuck up on her almost overnight. Now stop with all this talk of heaven and white lights, and lighten up. You're depressing me. I enclosed Lilly's obituary that Thelma sent me. Your oldest and most lovable friend, Mary P.S. Why don't you get another dog Em?

EMILY:

Because their lives are so temporary.

MARY:

All life is temporary. That's not the point. Emily, it's only love we're looking for sweet heart. So stop with all this gloomy stuff and let me remind you that I love you.

*   *   *

THELMA:

Dear Mary. Our Emily has always, for as long as we have known her, been somewhat of a delicate flower. Remember when we were seven and she howled when you sat on one of her invisible friends? Now, I might be getting this wrong, but I remember that you told her that you were terribly sorry for squashing her little imaginary buddy but you didn't see him sitting there. When she kept crying you told her to stop wailing and just muster up another friend. She can't help it Mar, it's just the way that God made her. Besides when you get to be our age, who doesn't think about death?

*   *   *

EMILY:

Dear Mary. You are not going to believe this. Elmer Carmichael asked our Thelma to marry him! He got down on one knee and proposed with a half-carat diamond ring that he bought at Walmart. After Thelma said yes he started to cry. And then Thelma had to dial 911 because he couldn't get off the floor. The paramedics had to pry that old Elmer up off the floor. And, are you ready for this Mar? Thelma's granddaughters call the happy couple – Thelmer.

THELMA:

Mary, the wedding will be on Valentine's Day. The reception will be at the Veteran's Club. I can almost hear you cackling with delight Mary Ann Marie. I will be eighty years old this year and I'm acting like a teenager. Who ever heard of people this old getting married? This is ridiculous. Love…Thelmer

*   *   *

MARY:

Thelma, I think you and Elmer Carmichael are as cute as a bug's ear together.

EMILY:

Dear Thelma, it was a beautiful ceremony. I don't think there was a dry eye in the Veteran's Club when Elmer made the toast to his new bride. You looked radiant Thel.

THELMA:

Oh for goodness sake. I hardly looked radiant. You're a dear for saying so Em. But it was a beautiful ceremony.

MARY:

Dear Emily. Elmer Carmichael is just a husk of a man isn't he? Poor old coot – looks like he's about to keel over. Speaking of old coots, Ma sends her love.

* * *

EMILY:

Happy Birthday Mary! How does it feel to be that old?

MARY:

Besides the fact that I'm eighty years old and I still live with my mother, I would say life is grand!

* * *

THELMA:

Dear Mary. It was wonderful speaking with you last night. Elmer says he can always tell when I'm on the telephone with you or Emily because of all the laughing that I do. I love taking our trips down memory lane to the old days in Lark Eden. Let's face it Mar, people as old as us have nothing left to do *but* remember do we? I spend most of the day looking back at the moments of my life, all of those people that have faded away. I only sleep about four hours a night, so I guess I also spend the hours of darkness looking at the faded faces of my life. There doesn't seem to be much of a present any more, does there? God bless you Mary Ann Marie. I love you to pieces.

MARY:

Thelma, what is all this about fading faces? You sound perfectly morbid my friend. You have a beautiful family, children, grandchildren, and great grandchildren, and a new husband. You're a newlywed for Pete's sake. An eighty-one year old newlywed! Now surely that is something to celebrate. Do me a favor the next time you want to write all this morose stuff, write it to Emily. She would love it. As for me, I'm enjoying my golden years here at the House of Happy.

*   *   *

EMILY:

Dear Thelma. I'm writing this to you from the car. Warren is driving and I had to get this down before I saw you. In a few hours I will see you and I don't know what I will say to you. To lose a child is something that I cannot… Thelma, I remember the day that Paul was born like it was yesterday. I know that he didn't have an easy time of things after Vietnam. That war killed him Thelma. His death is a loss that is unspeakable. Thelma, I'm afraid that I don't have the words of comfort for you. I love you dear friend.

*   *   *

MARY:

Emily, I just got off the phone with Elmer. He said that Thelma is doing all right considering the circumstances. To be honest, it's him that I'm worried about. He is older than dirt – the old coot. If anything were to happen to him I don't know if Thelma could take it. I've called her every day since Paul's funeral and told her how much I love her and that I'm thinking about her. Shit, Em I can't help it, but I'm so damn mad at Paul for doing this. How could he kill himself knowing that his eighty-two year old God-fearing mother would have to live with it? I just thank God that she has that old geezer Elmer there to look after her.

*   *   *

THELMA:

My Dearest Mary. I am writing to thank you for your lovely sympathy card. Elmer Carmichael was a good man, God rest his dear old soul. As you know, I believe that God has a plan and He must have known that I would need Elmer after Paul's death. God sent me that gentle old man for a reason. I only got to be his wife for a few short years but I feel blessed to have had the honor of being married to such a kind, loving creature. On his deathbed he said that he was glad it was him who was going first because he knew that I had you and Emily to watch after me. May that dear man rest in peace. Love, Thelmer

*　　*　　*

EMILY:

Dear Mary. Do you think Thelma will be all right? She lost her son and her husband within a matter of months.

MARY:

Don't worry Em. She'll be all right.

*　　*　　*

EMILY:

Are you okay Mary? You sounded horrible last night when I spoke to you.

MARY:

I'm fine Em. Don't you worry about me.

*   *   *

THELMA:

I miss my boy Mary. I know that I'm not supposed to question what our good Lord does, but I just can't understand why He took my boy. He was such a sweet child and he grew up to have so many troubles. Mary, I shudder when I think about what was going on inside his head. I'm so angry at myself for not seeing that he was in pain. Why didn't I see it Mary? I just wish I could have my boy back Mary. To tell that sweet child that I... To tell him that I know he was in pain. He was calling out for help and I just didn't hear him. I didn't hear him Mary. (cont'd)

*   *   *

THELMA:

Are you there Mary? Did you get my letter? (cont'd)

*   *   *

THELMA:

Mary are you there?

MARY:

I'm here Thelma.

THELMA:

Oh thank goodness, I was worried.

MARY:

Thelma, watch after Emily May – your daughter Emily. I think she needs you. And Rita, I worry about her too. Take care of them Thelma.

*   *   *

EMILY:

You did the right thing Mary. You have spent your entire life taking care of her. From the time you were a little girl you have been the one who was always there for her. She needs more than you can give her now. From what Thelma tells me it sounds like a pretty nice place she'll be living. It's time to let go Mary.

MARY:

The place smells like soup Emily.

EMILY:

You did the right thing.

MARY:

She's madder than an old wet hen Em. Says I'm sending her away to die. Em, I'm so tired of listening to her drone on about how awful everything is. I'd like to stick a piece of duck tape over her mouth.

EMILY:

You're a good daughter Mary.

MARY:

Em, I never told you this – but years ago, after Franklin Harding – I took the wedding dress that Ma got me to the Goodwill on Whitesburg Drive here in Huntsville. I needed to get rid of it Em. And then – every day after work, I walked home, down Hogan Drive, and then left onto Weatherly Road. And then instead of turning left toward home, I turned right onto Whitesburg Drive just to be able to see the dress hanging in the window. It just hung there, like some sort of ghost. And every day for the next four months when I turned right onto Whitesburg Drive I hoped – hoped that the dress would be gone. I wanted so badly for someone to buy it, to wear it. And then one day – it was gone. And I imagined a church, and a wedding, and bridesmaids. And over the years I found myself imagining what her life might have been like, and the house she might have lived in and the family that she might have had.

EMILY:

Mary stop.

MARY:

And then a few weeks ago I was cleaning out Ma's room and I found a box under the bed. I accidently knocked it with the vacuum – and there it was. It was the dress Em. The lace was yellowed and the little bows on it were all smashed down and frayed at the edges. Em – Ma was the one who bought the…

EMILY:

Mary stop.

MARY:

Look at me Em, carrying on like a crybaby. I'm just a silly old woman. Just a silly…

*   *   *

THELMA:

Mary dear, Emily told me that your mother is doing well at Sunnybrook. How are you dear? I haven't heard from you...

EMILY:

Mary why haven't you called me back?

THELMA:

Don't you have an answering machine Mary? The phone just rings and rings...

EMILY:

Please call Mary.

MARY:

I'm fine ya'll. Just enjoying the peace and quiet. Have I mentioned how quiet it is here without Ma flapping her jaw.

EMILY:

Oh thank goodness. Don't you do that again Mary. I worry terribly when I don't hear from you.

* * *

MARY:

Ten more days!

THELMA:

And counting!

EMILY:

Thelma, Mary's flight gets in at 9:05 and then yours gets in at 11:00 so we'll meet you outside of baggage claim. My car is the one with the bumper sticker that reads: I'M NOT DRIVING THIS WAY TO PISS YOU OFF.

THELMA:

Imagine I'm eighty-four years old and I'm getting on an airplane for the first time in my life!

MARY:

Better late than never Thel.

EMILY:

Nine more days!

MARY:

Carnival Cruise Lines here we come!

THELMA:

Eight more days girls! I love you both to pieces.

EMILY:

I'm so excited I can barely contain myself.

THELMA:

Seven more days!

MARY:

Six.

EMILY:

Oh girls, last night I looked over at Warren sleeping in his chair, and then after I checked to see if he was breathing, I just started crying. I couldn't stop. But it wasn't because I was sad. It was because in just a few short days I will be on a ship in the middle of the ocean with my oldest and best friends in the world.

MARY:

Bless your pea pickin' heart.

THELMA:

Five more days.

EMILY:

Four.

MARY:

Abyssinia!

THELMA:

Three.

EMILY:

Two.

THELMA:

Mary?

EMILY:

Are you there, Mary?

THELMA:

Mar?

*   *   *

EMILY:

Dear Mrs. Able. I have written many letters in my life and yet I find myself…

THELMA:

And yet I find myself struggling to find the words to express how much…

EMILY:

I miss Mary.

THELMA:

I know this may sound crazy, but I want so badly to pick up the phone and call her…

EMILY:

To pick up a pen and write to her.

THELMA:

You see Mary was the person that I told everything to…

EMILY:

And as strange as this may sound – I find myself wanting to tell her about her own death.

THELMA:

It's hard to believe …

EMILY:

That your daughter and I have known each other for eighty years.

THELMA:

She didn't tell Emily and me that she was sick…

EMILY:

I can only imagine that she didn't want to worry me…

THELMA:

After what I've been through recently.

EMILY:

Year after year things come undone, and yet my friendship with Mary always stayed intact.

THELMA:

Many people that I have loved have passed...

EMILY:

It hasn't always been easy for me to believe. Yet I have always believed in one thing...

THELMA:

I've lost two husbands and a child. And yet I have found the strength to keep on. And now for the first time in my life I don't know how I will keep on. I realize now that it isn't God who deserves all the credit for...

EMILY:

Mary once said that it's only love we're looking for. Now I finally understand what she meant...

THELMA:

I realize now the Lord's ways aren't as mysterious as one might believe, either that or I finally figured out the mystery...

EMILY:

She meant that love is the only thing we can really believe in. Mrs. Able I loved your daughter...

THELMA:

I am so deeply thankful that your daughter was in my life…

EMILY:

I have never believed in the shapes of familiar people loping around a white heaven. But I hope that Mary can hear me now…There is place where the lark sings…

THELMA:

The Lord has a purpose…

EMILY:

It's a place between all it is that you hope for and all it is that you have. Between tomorrow and today. Between dream and wake…

THELMA:

I know now that I am who I am because of Mary. God's purpose for me was Mary.

EMILY:

This is the place where the song of the larks can be heard in our Eden.

THE END

9 781935 961079